Clyde and Susanna, The
Who Always Loved Her Shine

by Kymberli Dyson

Illustrated by Patricia Suzanne Murray

this little light™

Dedicated to our loving families and friends
and to all the children whose "light" is true beauty.

Other titles published in the this little light series:
Clyde, The Cloud Who Always Cried

Copyright Info. Et Al.
ISBN 1-885282-01-X

Printed in the U.S.A. ■ First printing, 1995

Once upon a time, there was a cloud named Clyde. Clyde is still known as the cloud who always cries.

Clyde's old tears came from jealousy,

he was envious of the sun. The sun's name

is Susanna and tells everyone she is #1.

Susanna is beautiful and boy
does she shine. She feels
she is the best,
the brightest and
all-around fine.

The other stars always tell

Susanna how pretty she is.

Susanna always replies, "I'm the Superstar

who should be in showbiz."

Marlon the moon likes the few moments

he is around Susanna, her heat makes him feel so good.

Susanna never compliments Marlon on anything she likes about him, like she should.

The birds love Susanna's beauty and
sing sweet melodies they make just
for her. Does Susanna thank the birds?
Why no, the thought just doesn't occur.

The flowers look up to Susanna, they know she helps them to grow. Susanna tells the flowers they wouldn't be beautiful if it wasn't for her lovely glow.

The birds, the moon, the flowers and stars

finally realized Susanna's not beautiful at all.

She is never nice to anyone — no one big or small.

They decided to go to Clyde
for help, they knew their
friend would understand.

Clyde listened to their complaints and went to God for a plan.

God knew Susanna had to change

her ways because her arrogance was getting too much to take.

God appreciated Clyde coming to Him for advice, knowing Clyde

didn't want to make a mistake.

God said, "I won't give you the answer for I feel you already know what to do. You had to learn a lesson and now Susanna needs to learn one too."

Clyde went back to the others and

told them Susanna should be ignored.

"Being alone all the time, she's sure to become bored."

The next morning Susanna is all aglow, assured this
is her prettiest day. She waits for her praises and listens
for what everyone is surely going to say.

Susanna waits and she waits, but her friends are not
to be found. She notices the silence and realizes even
the birds aren't making a sound.

Marlon the moon goes right by her, really on the go. The flowers never look up at her even for their daily "hello".

Susanna can't understand why
everyone is acting this way.
She says, "I will go visit Clyde
to see what he has to say."

Clyde said, "I'm sorry Susanna, but your vanity has you thinking you're the best in all the sky." "I didn't know it would make me lose my friends", she said as she started to cry.

Clyde said, "Beauty is how you act with your friends and everyone around you. Beauty is being kind, loving, and giving too."

Susanna realized Clyde was right and wanted to get rid of her pride. She went to her friends telling them she was sorry and wanted to be back at their side.

Susanna realized that beauty comes within, not just from what can be seen. Having friends is beautiful to her and she promised to try never to be mean.

Marlon, the flowers, the stars, and birds all welcomed Susanna back with cheers and shouts. They knew Susanna had changed, her overflowing love left no doubts.

Everyone is happy at how Susanna changed her ways. God can now make the sun truly beautiful as her love for others shines through her rays.